Sir Rhymesalot

Sir Rhymesalot

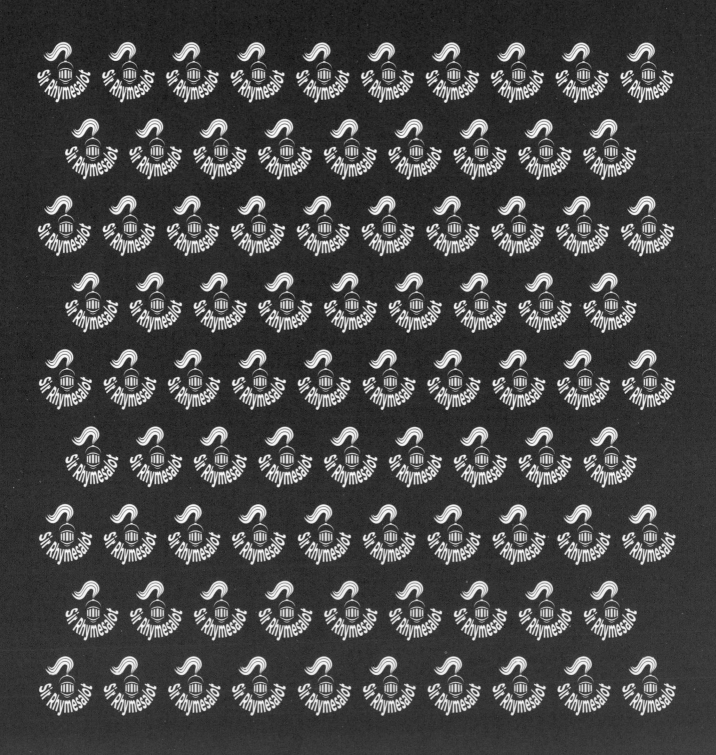

BETWEENERS

A very unsettling adventure

Sir Rhymesalot
Featuring the art of David Geiser

This book contains rhyming
Tools. Scan the QR code to
find out how they work.

While eating cornbread
on an outback camp bed
a voice from the sky gently whispered

My name is Ned
I'm a big floating head
Let me pull on your coat, he insisted

I cleared my throat,
"Pull on my coat?"
I questioned up into the sky.

"Yes", Ned went on,
"You see, where I'm from,
things have gone somewhat awry"

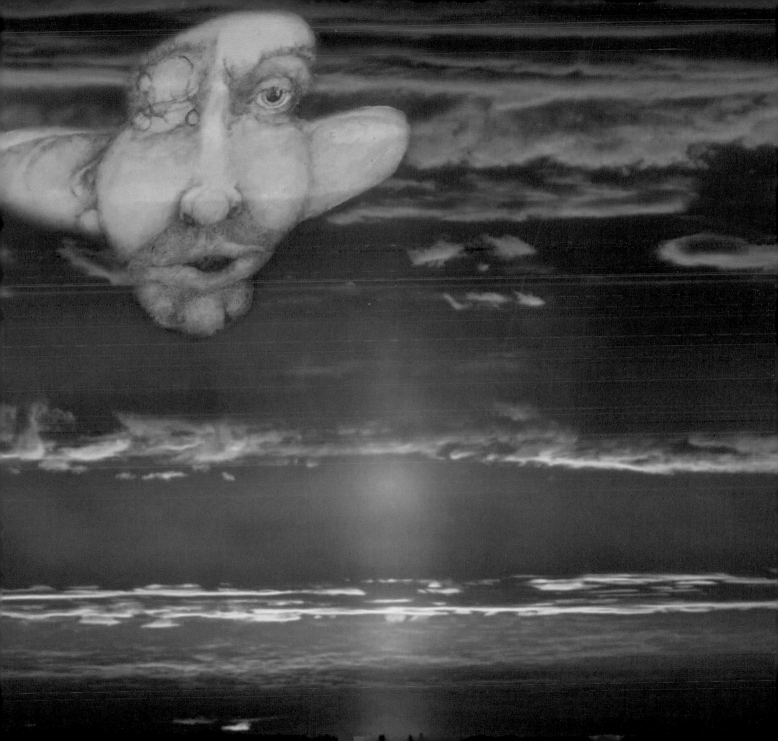

If you'd come along with me
you will very soon see
the predicament we find ourselves in

Don't dally or dither
simply jump hither
we'll zipooee to where you've not been

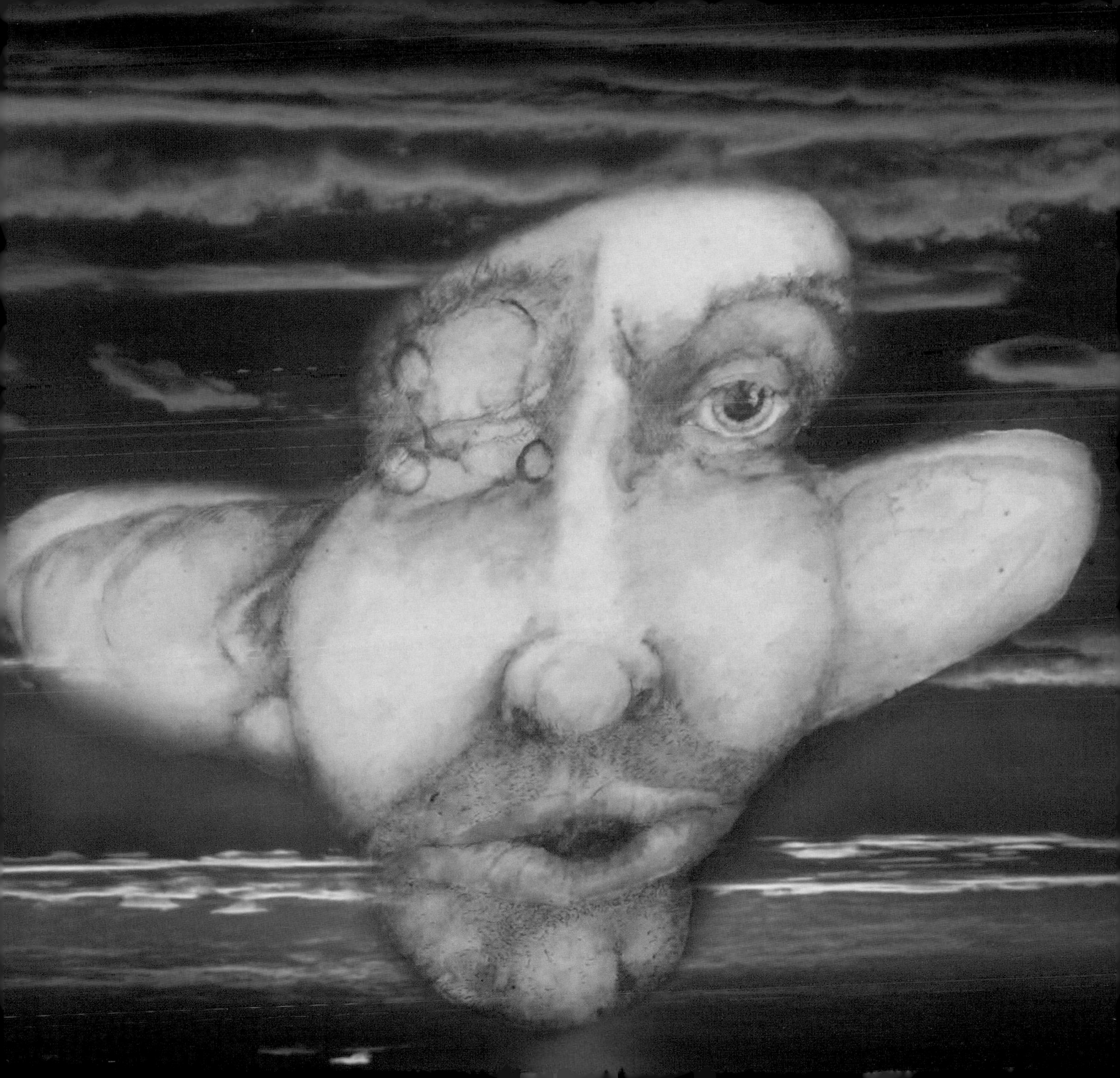

Before I could stay
we zipooee'd away
within seconds I was in an odd land

Surrounded by creatures
with unusual features
like a nose with a face on a hand

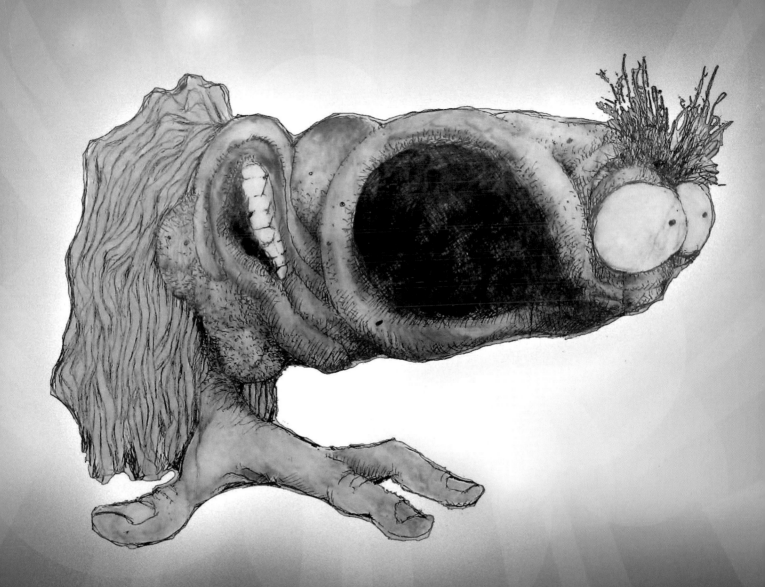

"Listen", said Ned
here's the problem, we're dead
and we realize it's not your intention

But your acts overwhelm
the spiritual realm
drastically affecting our dimension

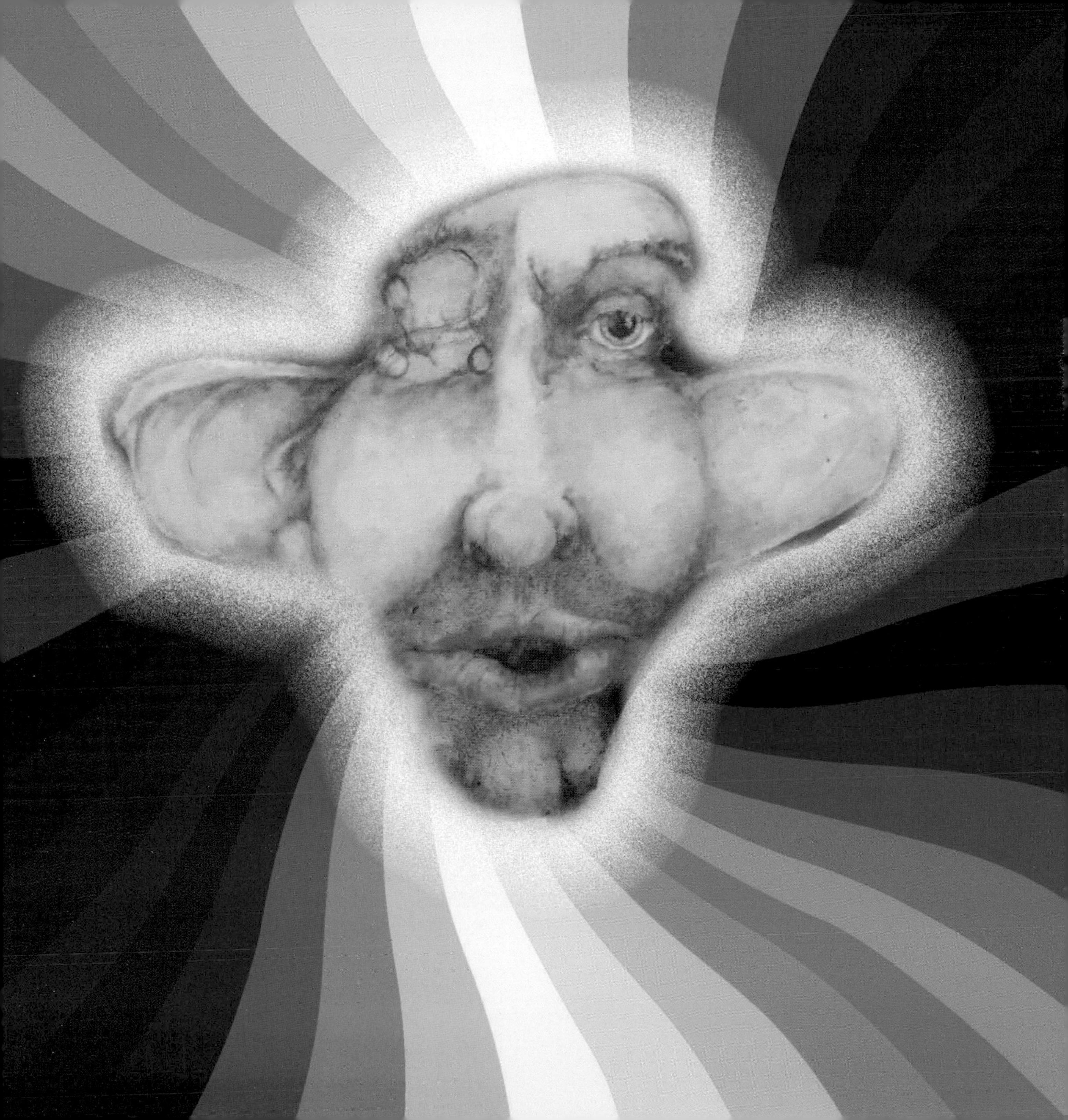

This is Frankie Four Lips
he's changed quite a bit
he used to look somewhat like **you.**

He woke up one year
with one giant ear
and four lips where there used to be **two.**

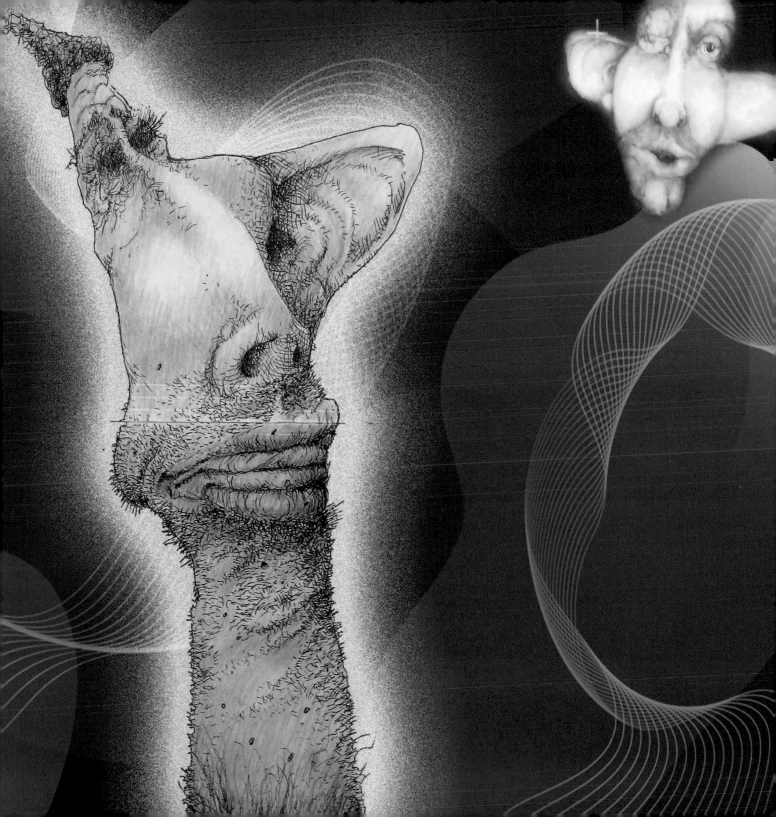

Then there's Rodney and Davo
they love to dance disco
their necks grow an inch every **month.**

If they extend any more
they'll be fourteen feet tall
and could view their own backs
from their **fronts**

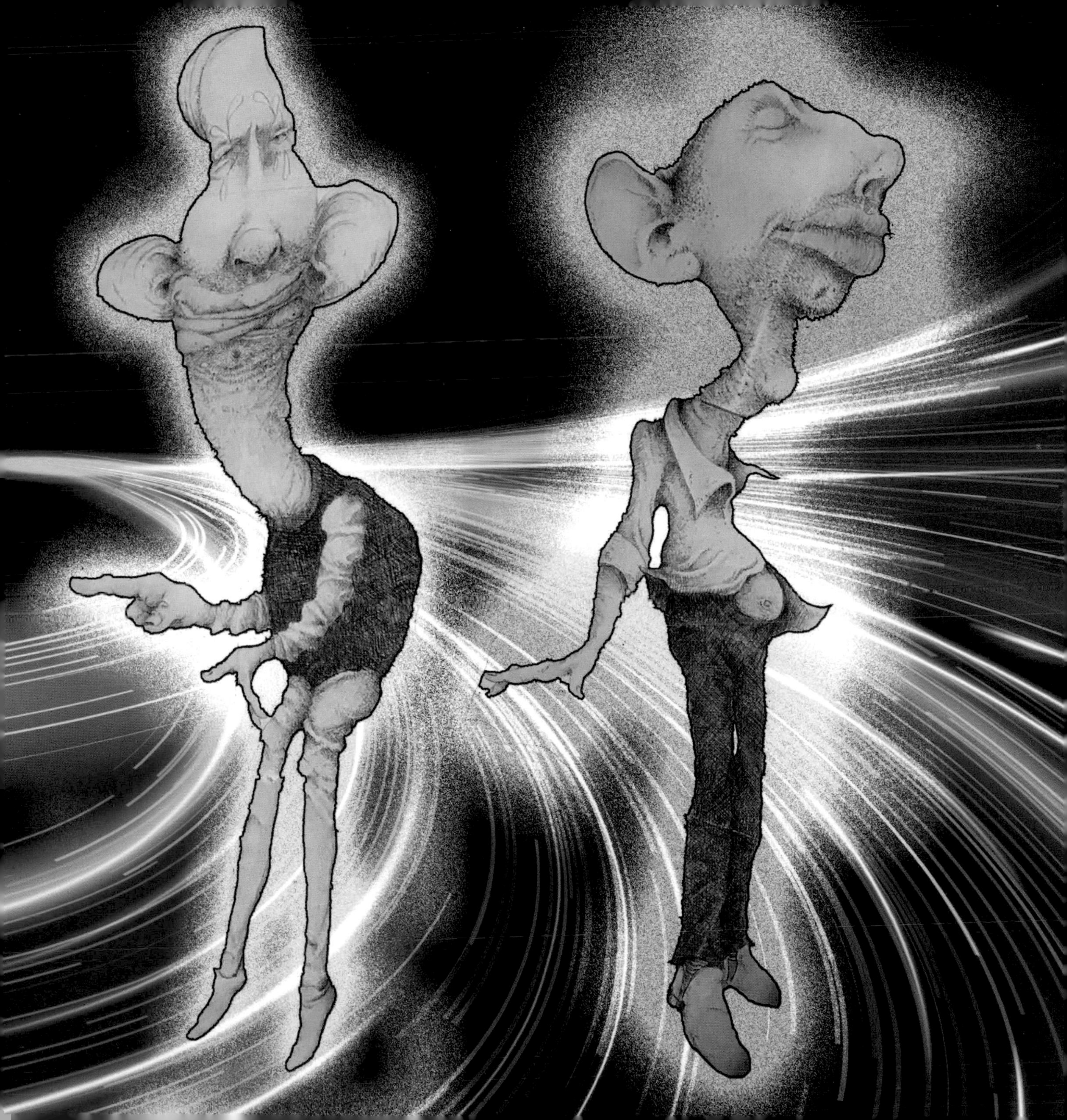

Tommy Tornado-Leg
had quite the pair of pegs
he used to love walks in the **park**

But his legs chose to funnel
and became a wind tunnel
devastating what laid in his **path**

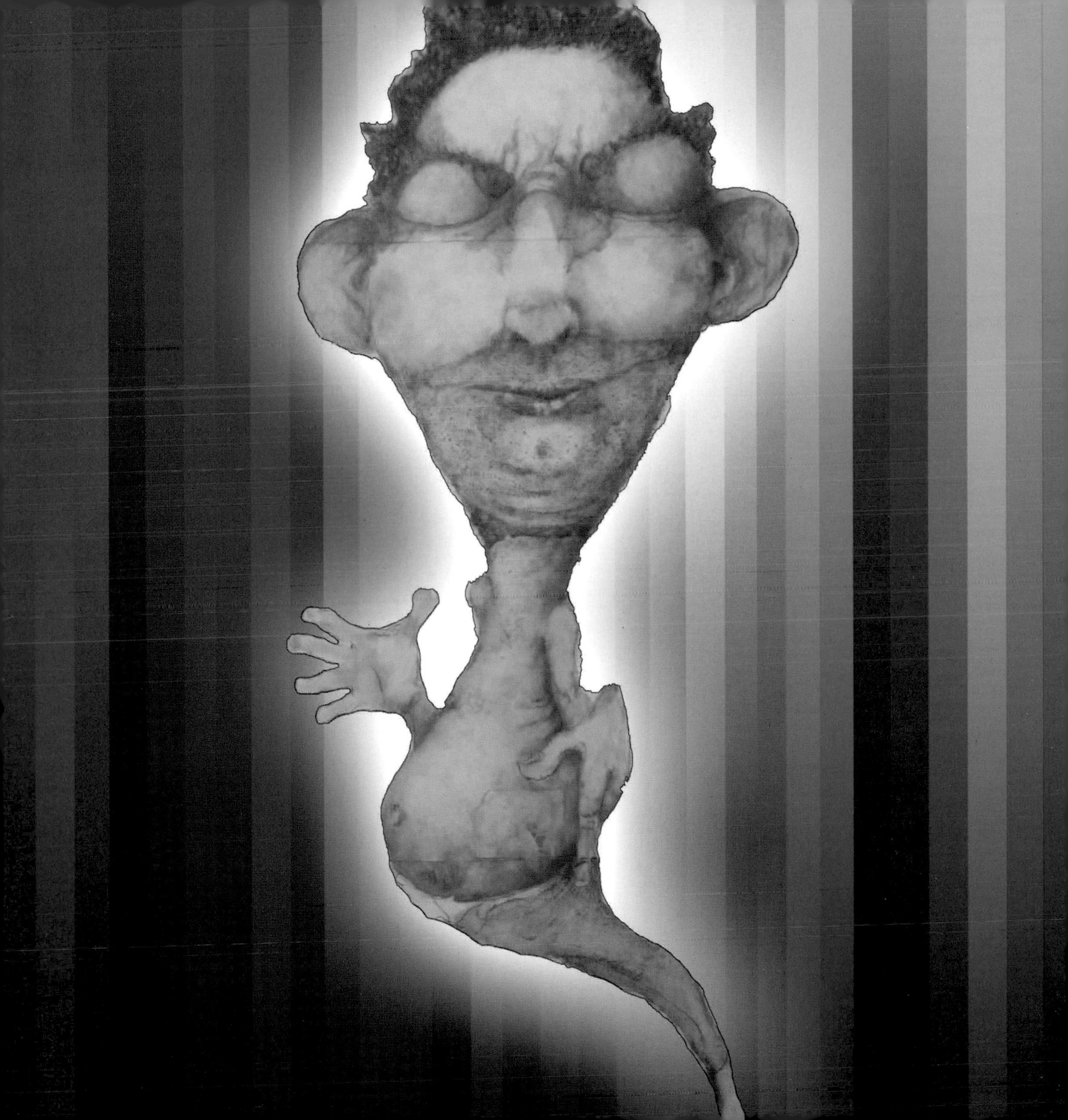

His shoulders are shrinking
and no longer winking
his eyeball moved into his neck

His arms are now twigs
as are his ribs
how tree-like will Mickie-Sticks get?

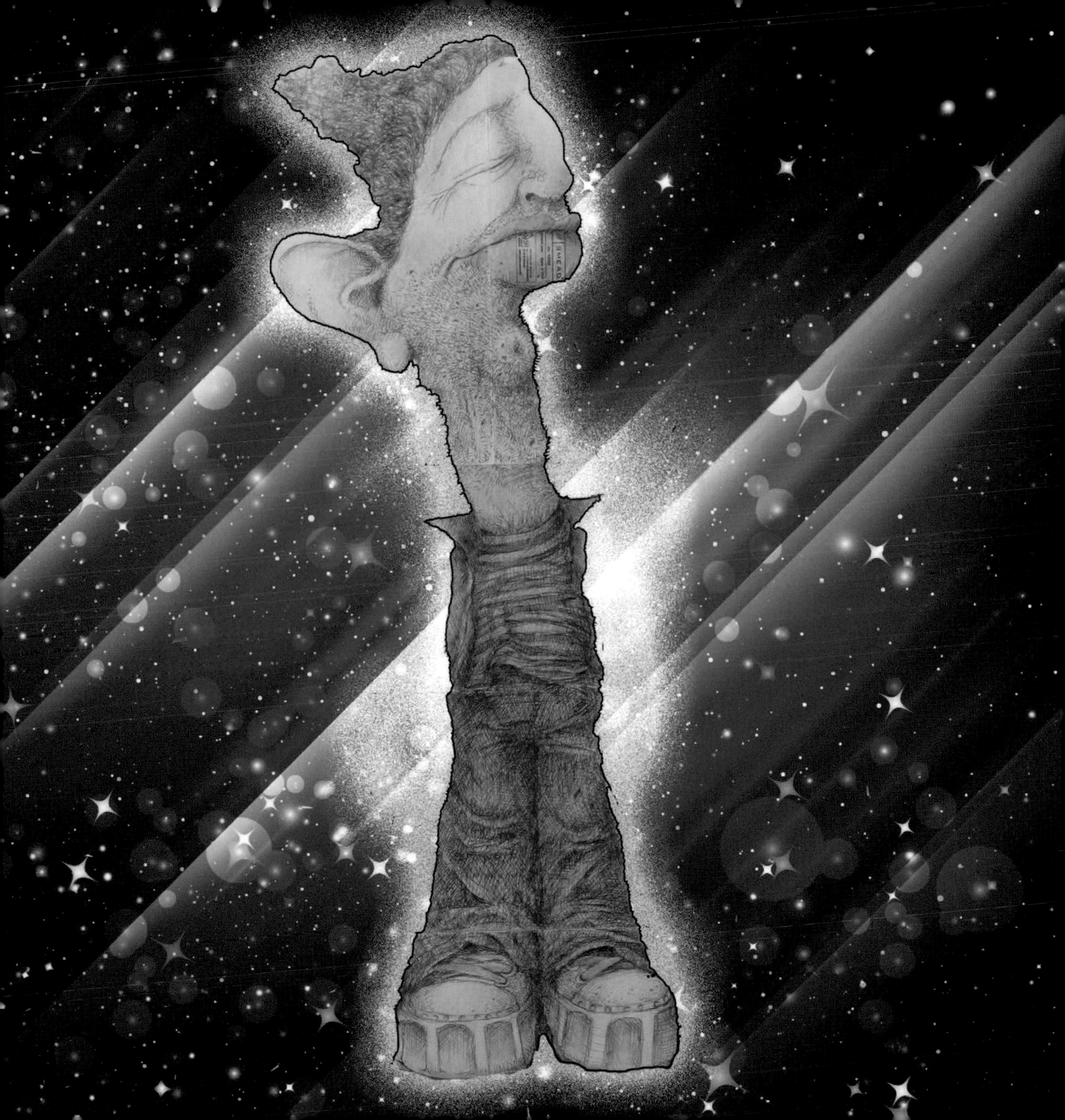

Sherry cherry-nose
has a mouse ear that grows
above her long flat noodly-neck

Her belly enshrouded
her fabulous trousers
Cherry-nosed Sherry's a mess

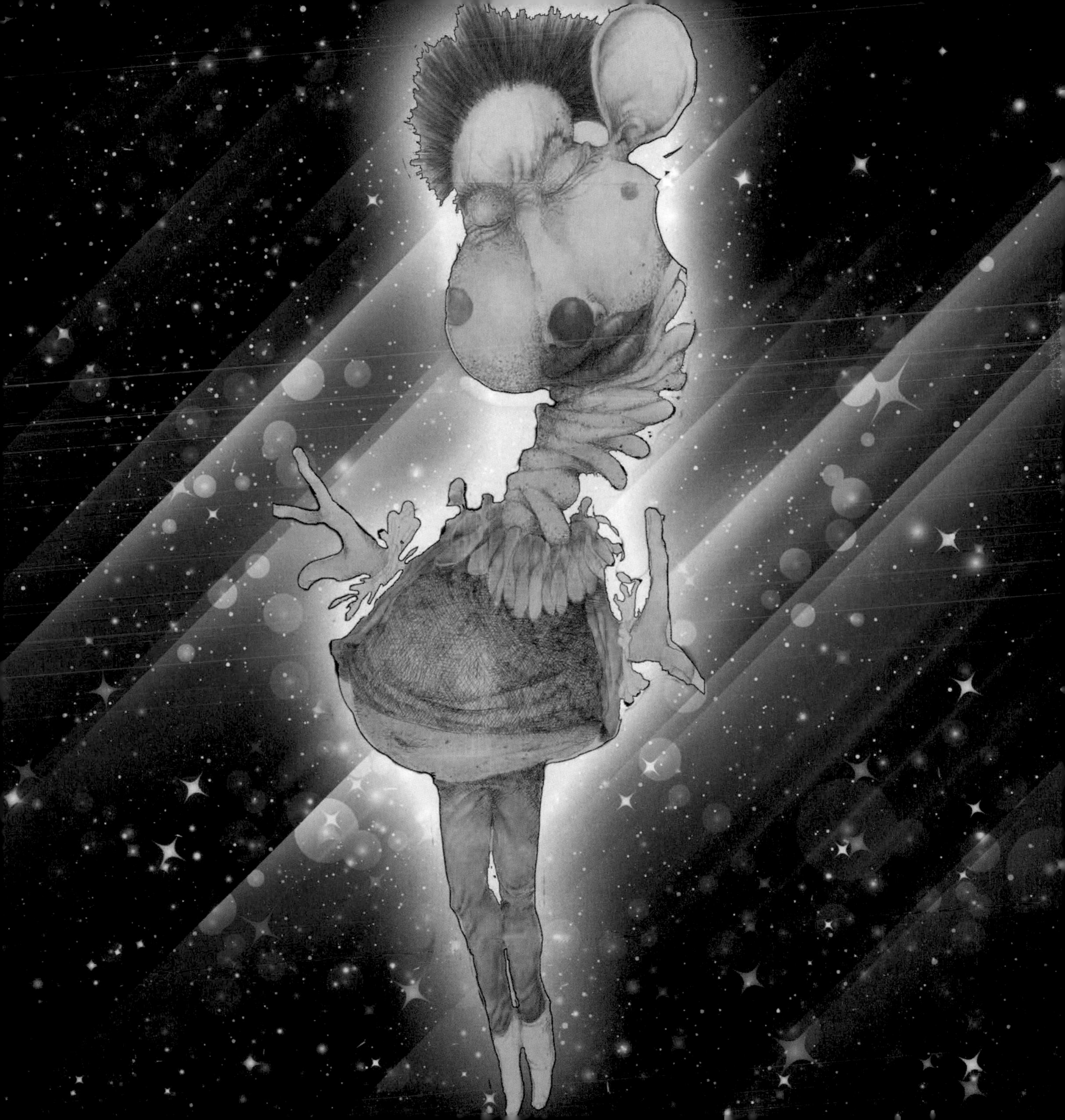

And Picksie's a dancer
his mauve stove-pipe pants are
permanently **pirouetting**

When his under-foot thins
the more that he spins
the deeper his pirouettes **get him**

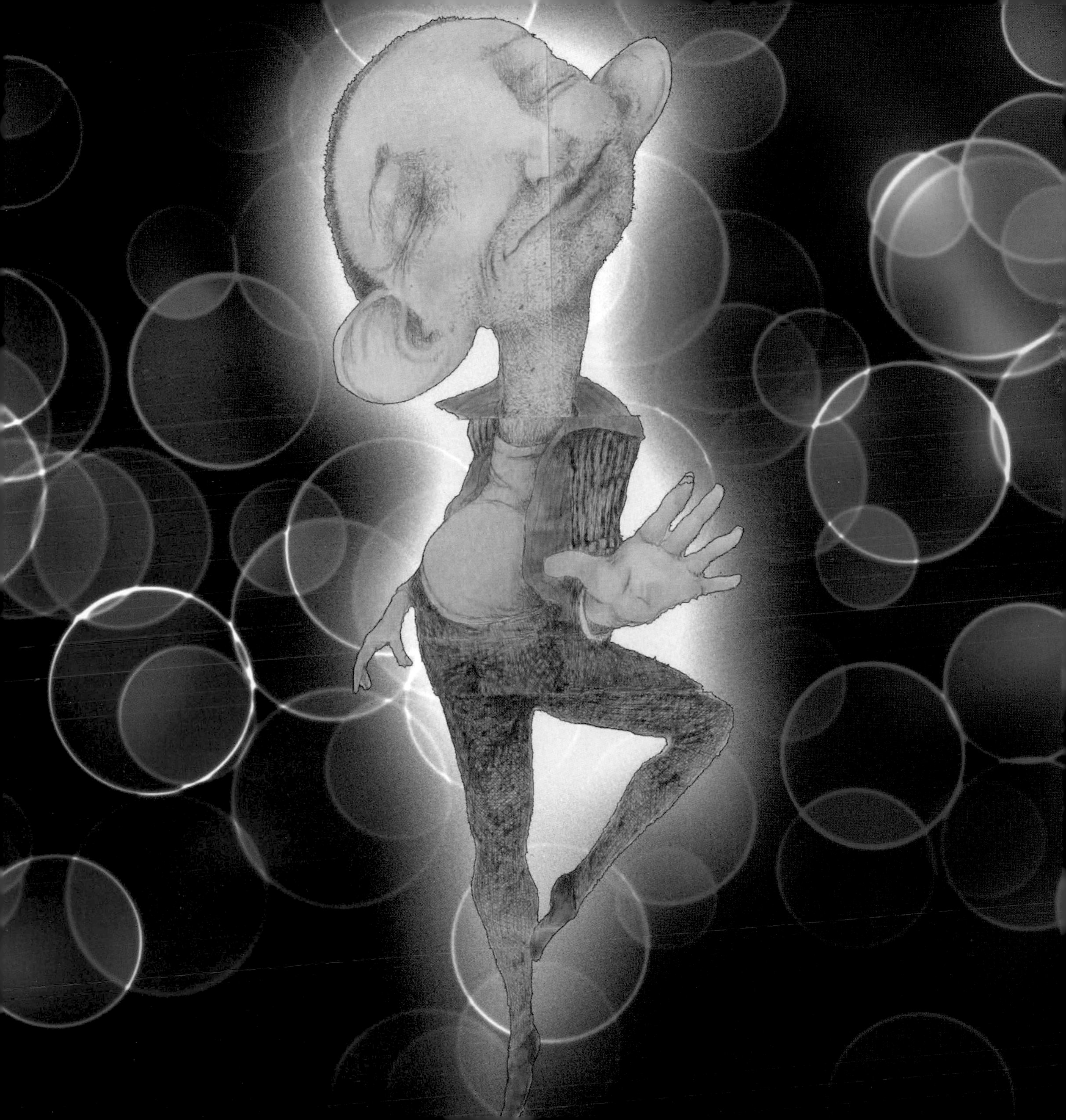

Sid was a circus clown
best side show clown around
right up until he went **nuts**

It all seemed quite fine
until two at a time
goblins flew out of his **guts**

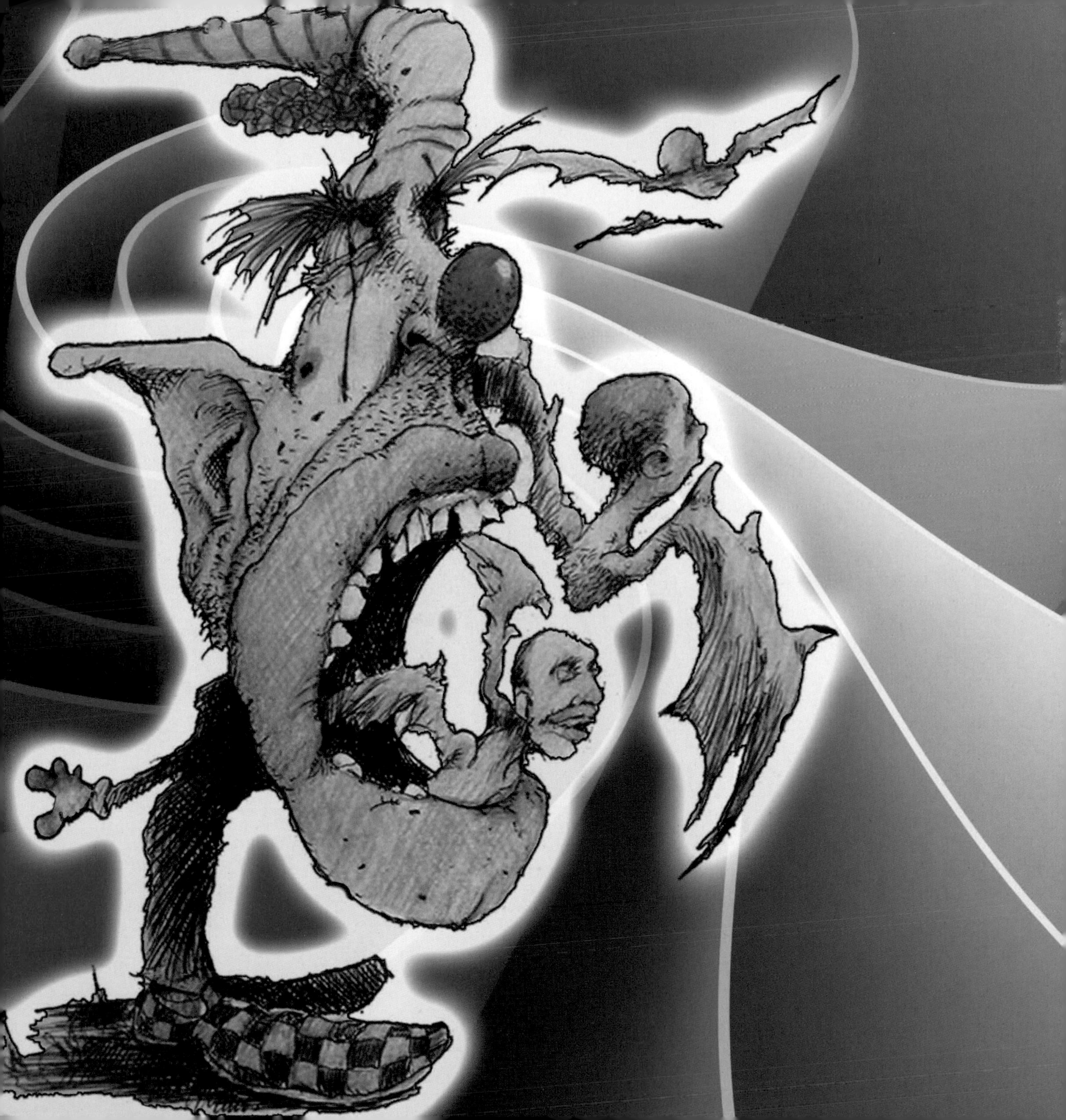

Septapus Max
makes very odd tracks
follow this fellow you can

His legs became hands
he's a true handy man
at once he can greet seven fans

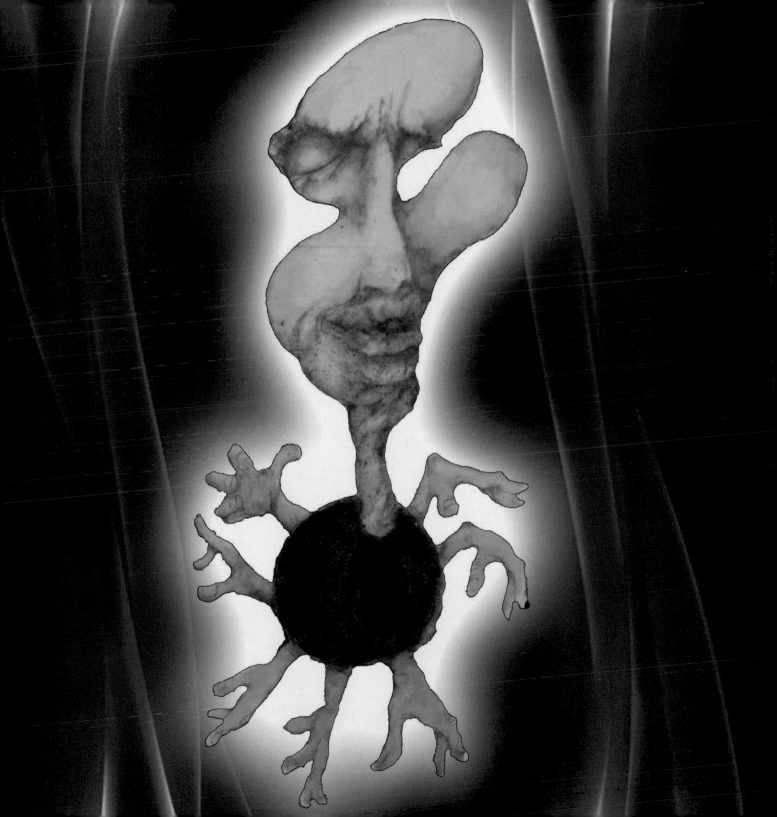

The McMurphy twins
were never this thin
they had quite the charm with the ladies

Then their arms disappeared
as did their beards
and their bodies turned into babies

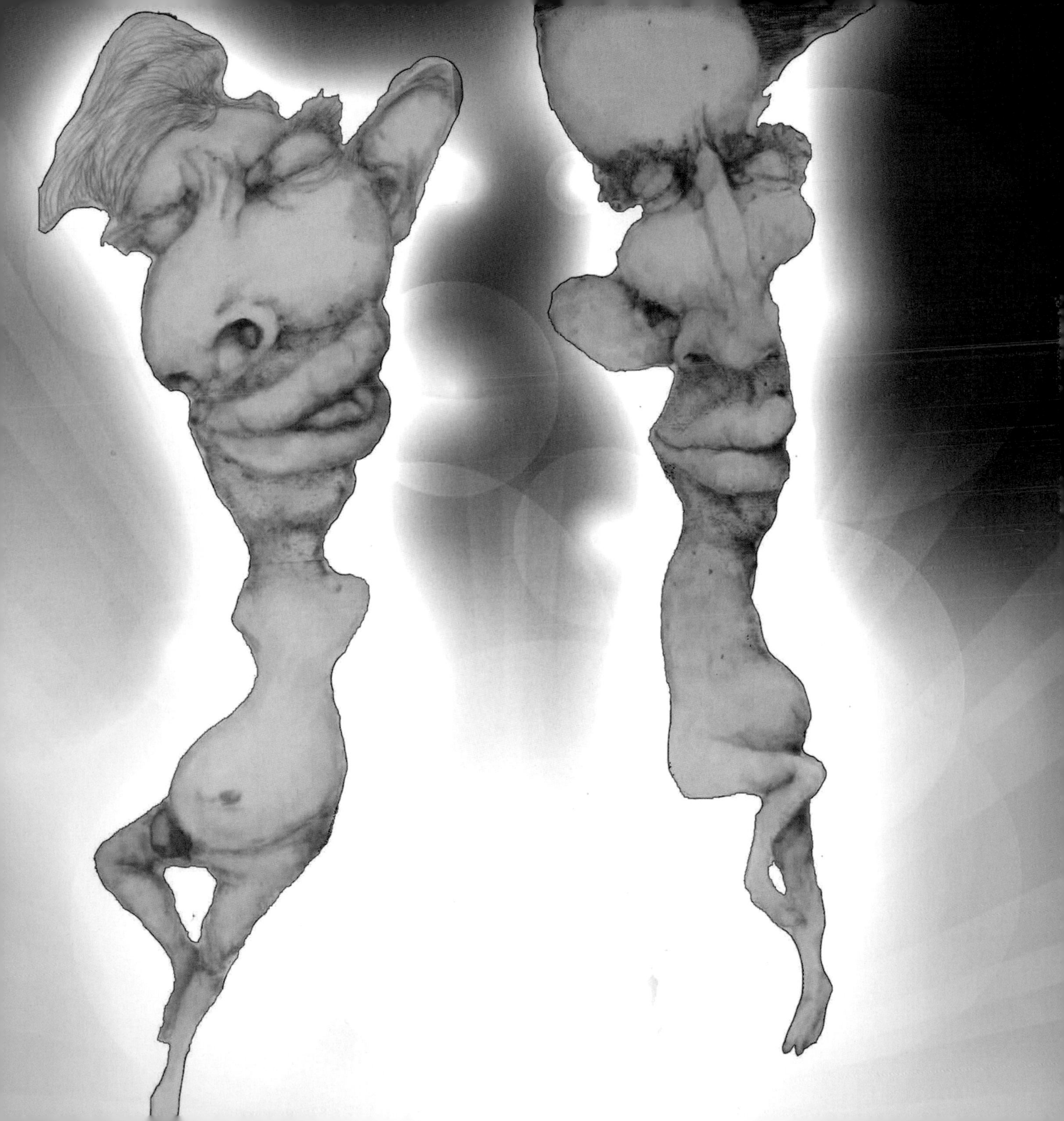

Laughing-Man Larry
was completely unwary
the first time he fell off his **feet**

He laughs endlessly
then **narcolepsy**
puts his back flat on the **street**

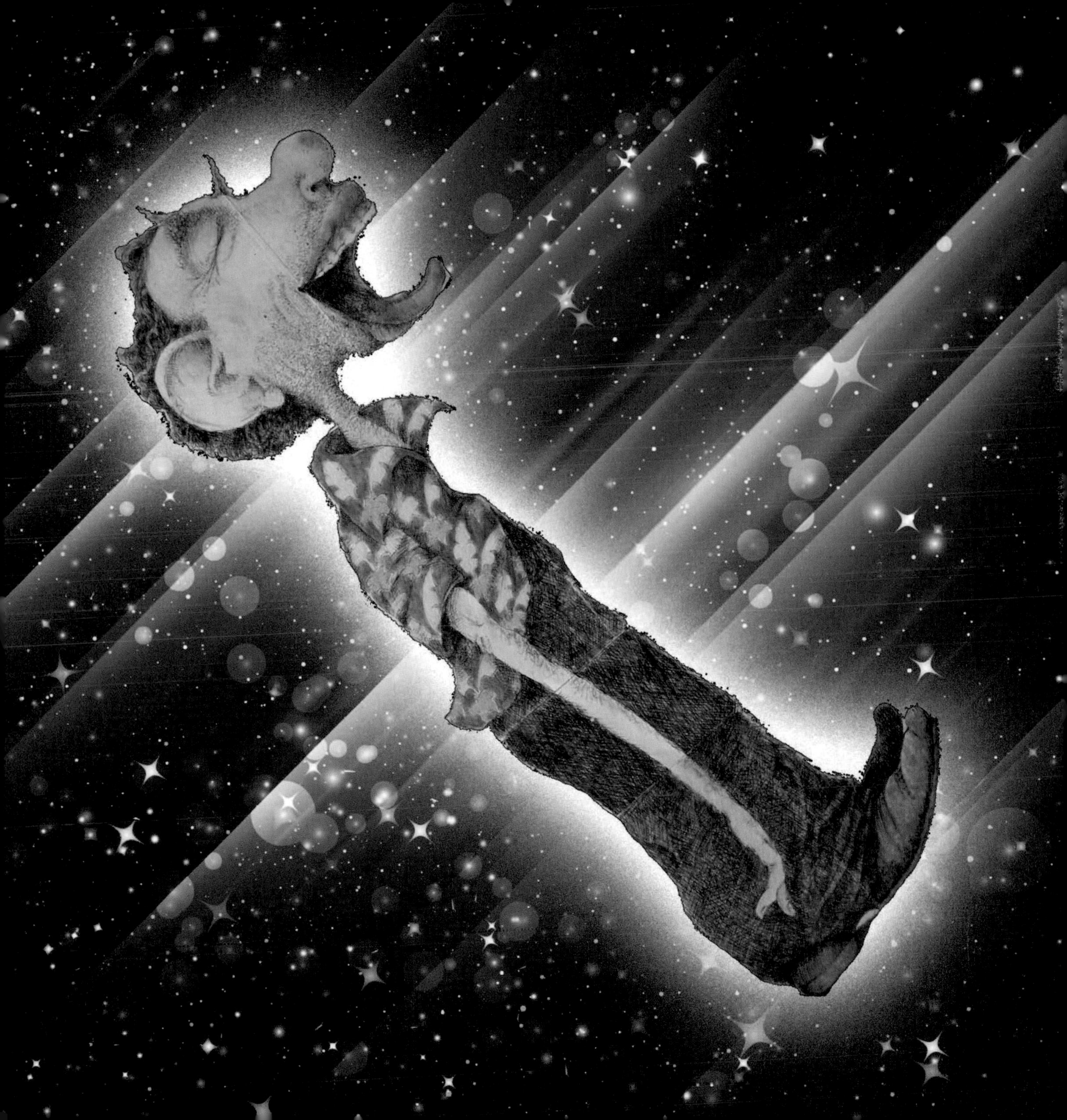

"So, why am I here"
I said in Ned's ear
what's causing this **transfiguration?**

"It's people, you **see**
the way that you **be**
your words have severe **causation"**

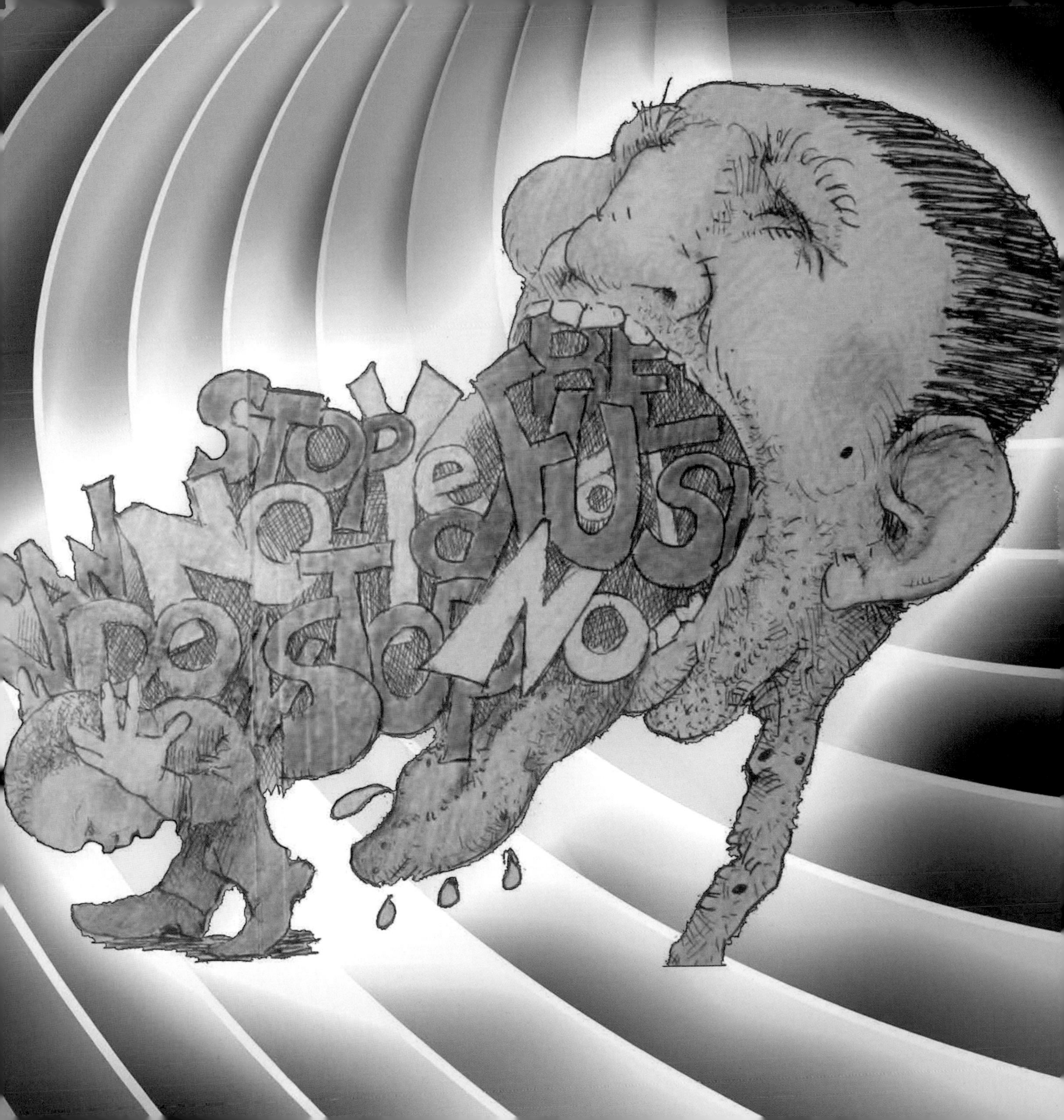
STOP

So much anger,
bitterness, and rage
it all ends up here in-**between**

Before they go back,
these souls are attacked
and when they go back, they are **fiends**

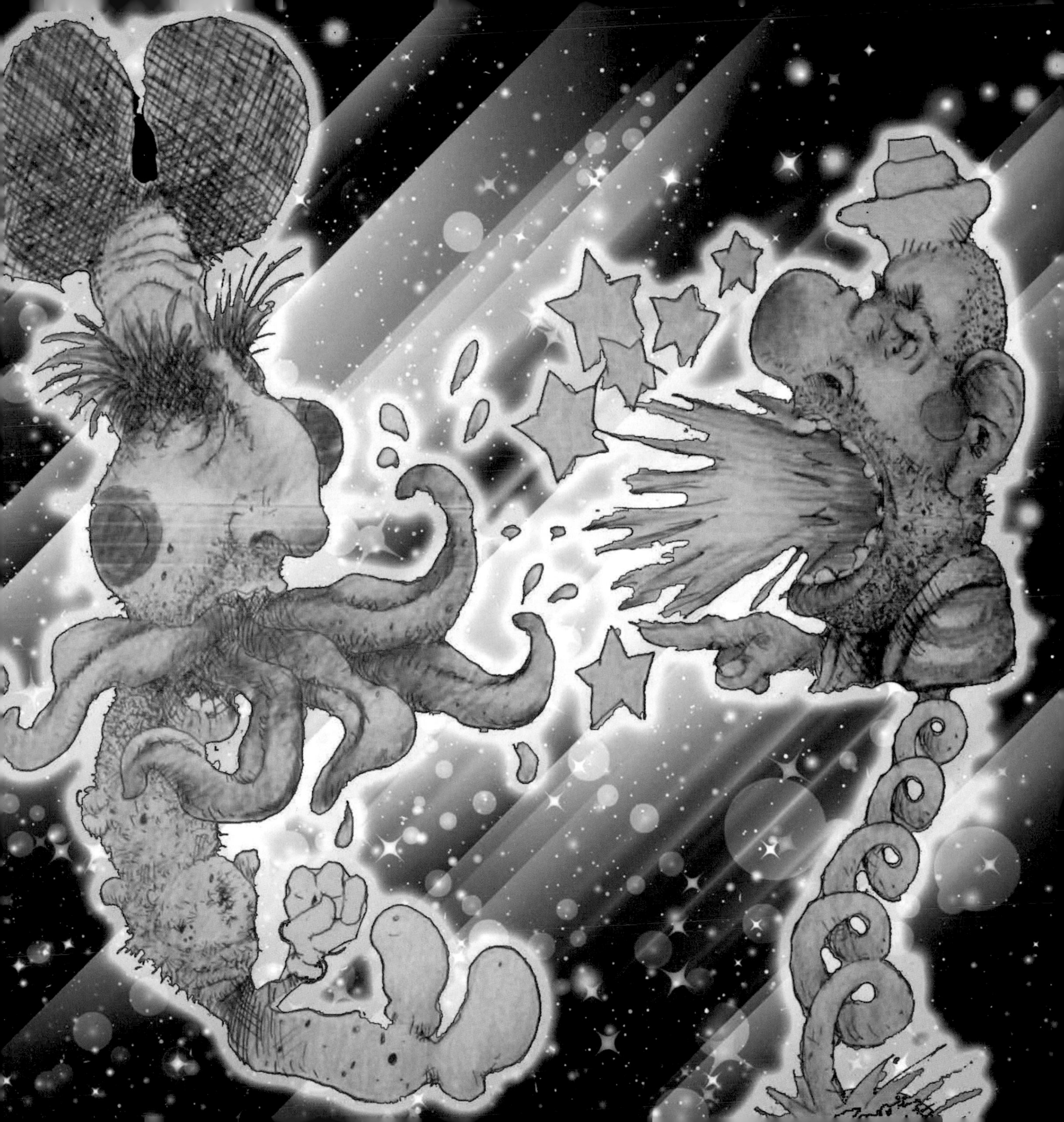

You'll need to act swiftly
lickedy splitly
too much time may have already **passed**

You have to think wider
don't be a snail rider
snail riders do tend to come **last**

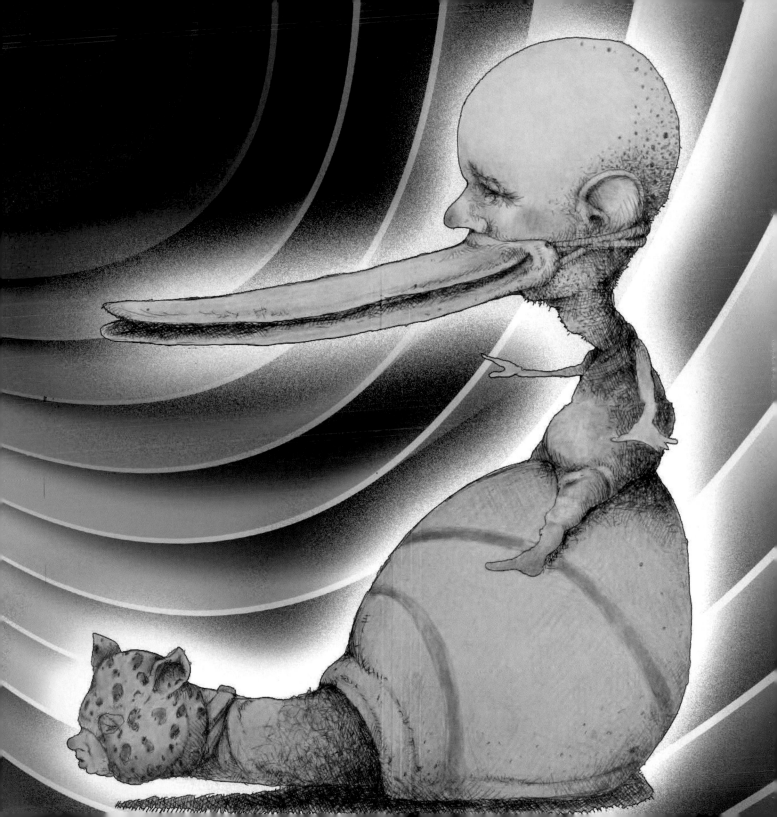

"So, what can I do?
how can I help?
I fear if I don't, we will **fail.**"

"You must tell the world
be respectful and kind
like a clown floating by on a **whale.**"

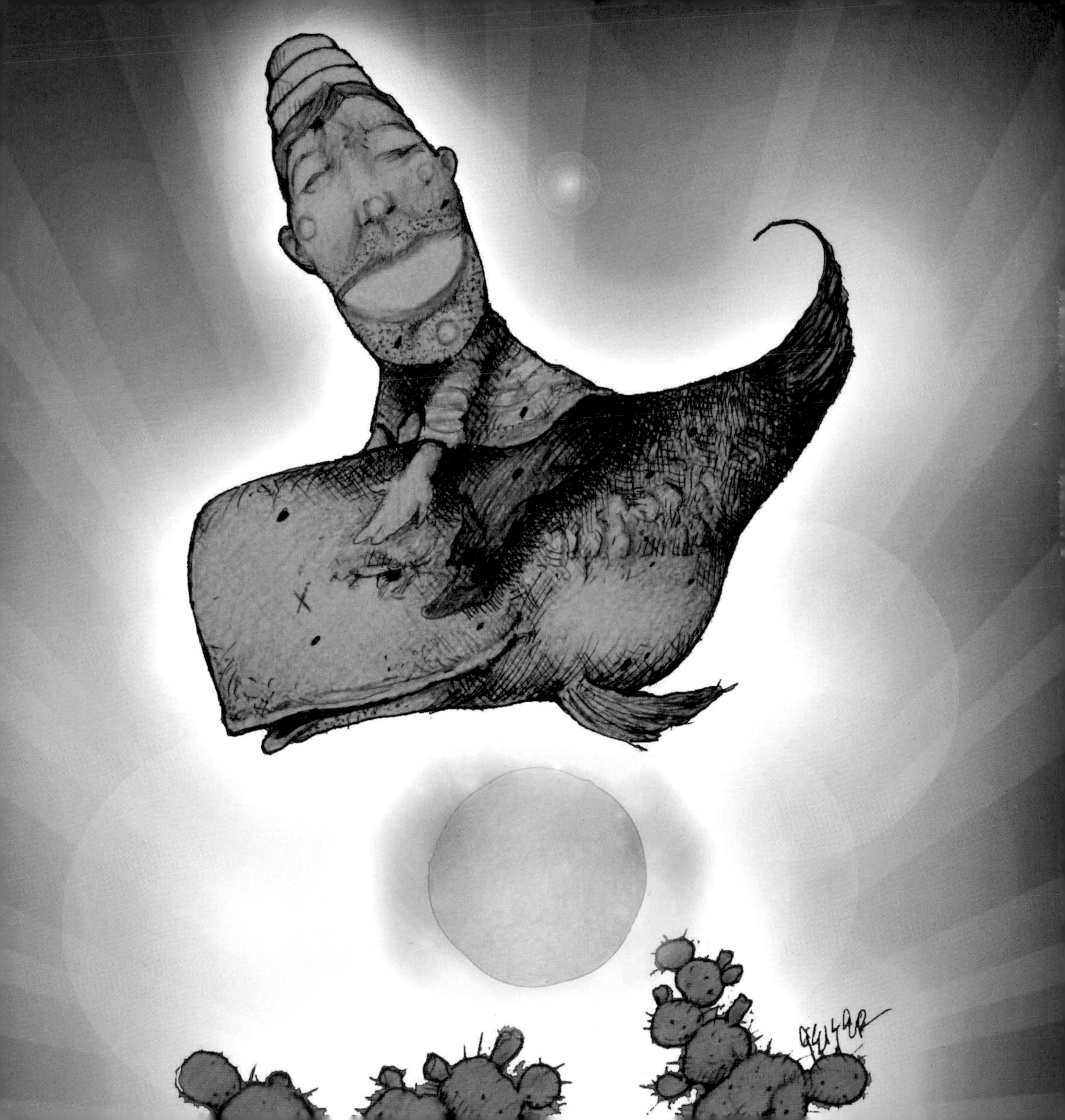

So, I'm here to say
we must change our ways
and stop being mean to each other.

If you continue
to grow the hate in you
we'll keep putting fiends into mothers.

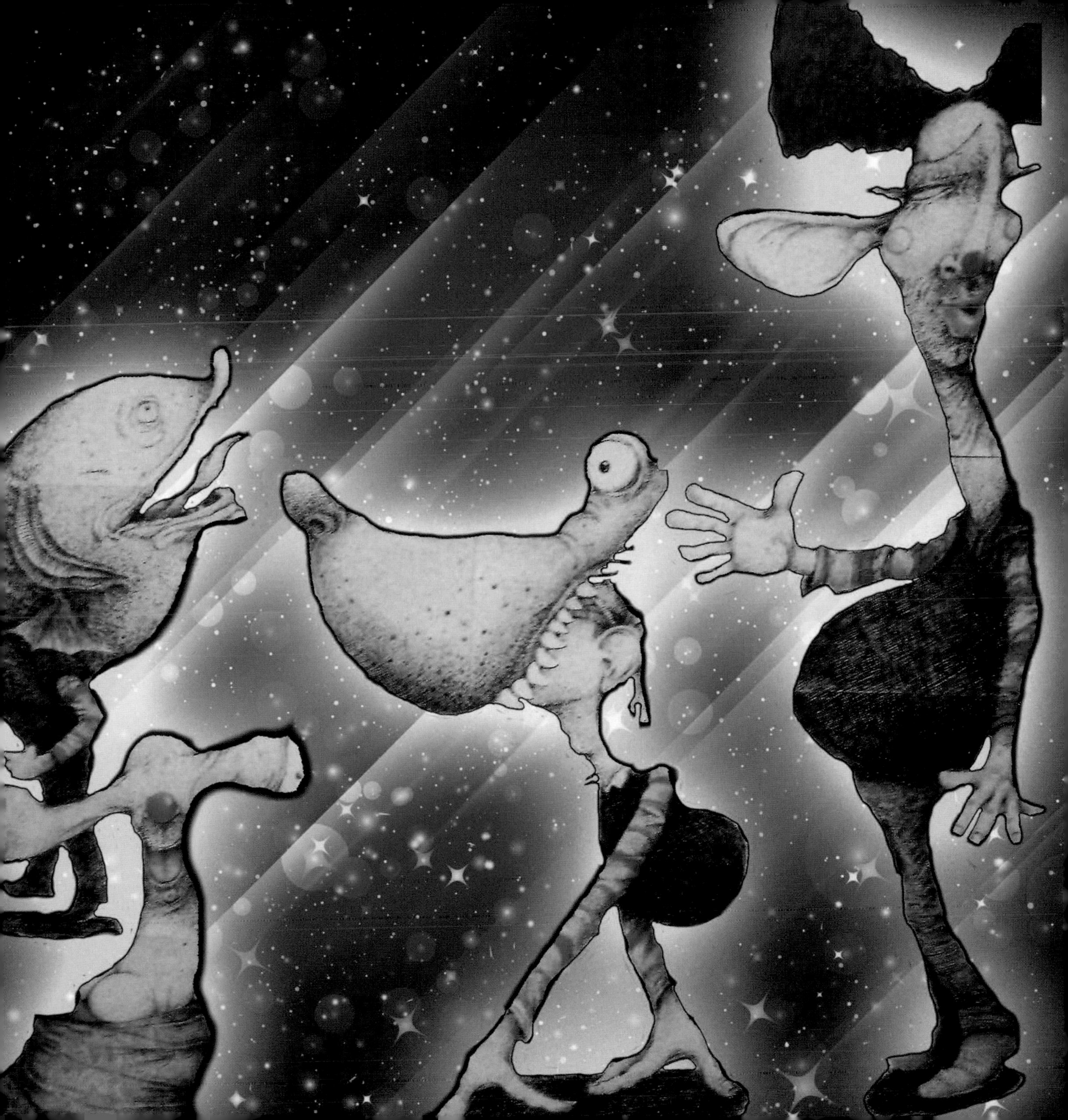

Scan this QR code with your phone camera
for more titles from imagine and wonder

PRINTED WITH SOY INK
Trademark of American Soybean Association

FSC www.fsc.org
MIX
Paper from responsible sources
FSC® C017606

ISBN: 9781953652553 (Hardcover)
Library of Congress Control Number: 2021933712

Your guarantee of quality

As publishers, we strive to produce every book to the highest commercial standards. The printing and binding have been planned to ensure a sturdy, attractive publication which should give years of enjoyment.

Replacement assurance

If your copy fails to meet our high standards, please inform us and we will gladly replace it.
admin@imagineandwonder.com

Printed in China by Hung Hing Off-set Printing Co. Ltd.

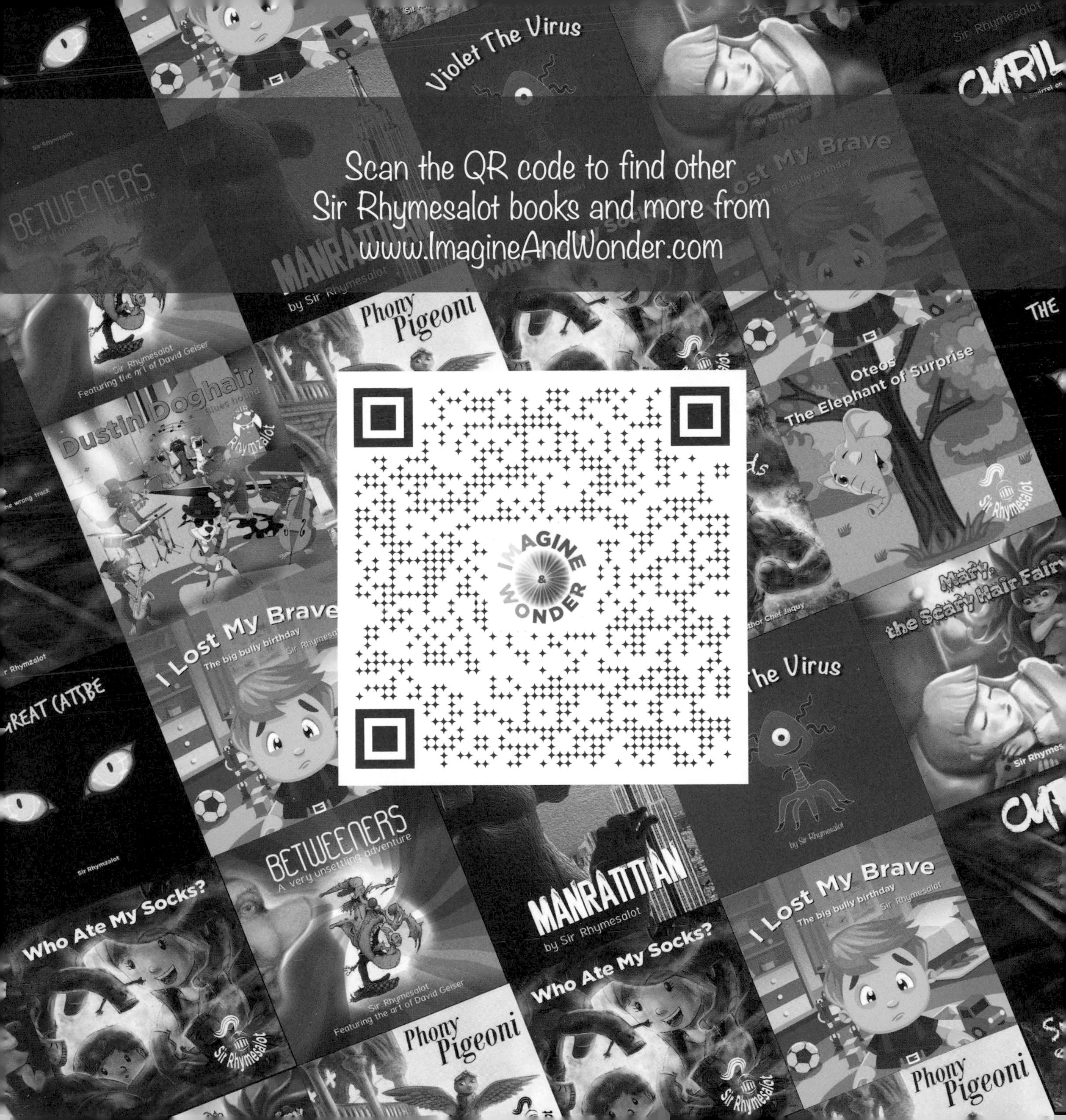
Scan the QR code to find other
Sir Rhymesalot books and more from
www.ImagineAndWonder.com
IMAGINE & WONDER
Violet The Virus
I Lost My Brave
The big bully birthday
Sir Rhymesalot
BETWEENERS
A very unsettling adventure
Sir Rhymesalot
Featuring the art of David Geiser
MANRATTTAN
by Sir Rhymesalot
Phony Pigeoni
Dustin Doghair
Blues hound
Oteos
The Elephant of Surprise
Mary, the Scary Hair Fairy
Who Ate My Socks?
Sir Rhymesalot

Sir Rhymesalot

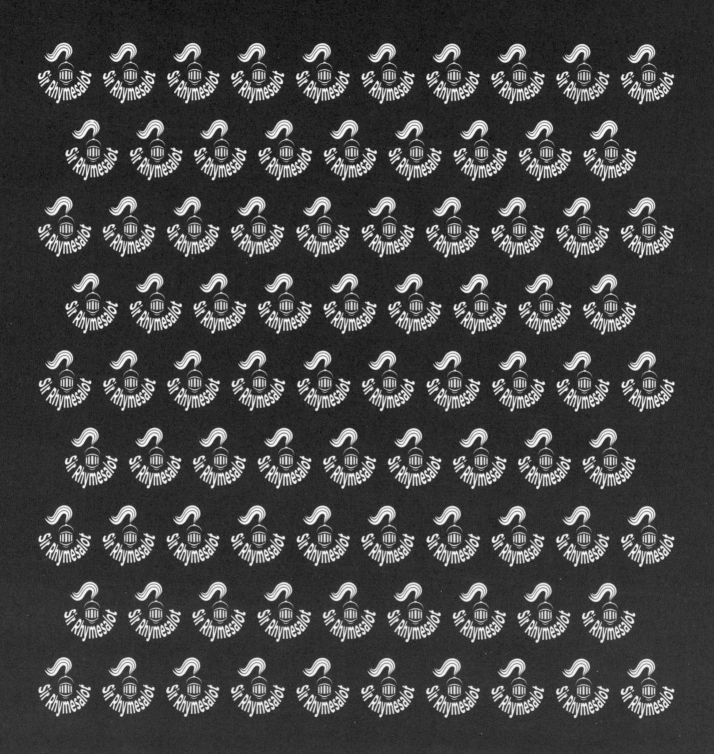